D1120256

LADYBIRD BOOKS, INC.
Auburn, Maine 04210 U.S.A.

LADYBIRD BOOKS, LTD.
Loughborough, Leicestershire, England

Copyright © 1992 Parachute Press, Inc.
New York, NY U.S.A.
All rights reserved. No part of this publication may be reproduced, stored in a retrieval
system, or transmitted in any form or by any means, electronic, mechanical,
photocopying, recording or otherwise, without the prior consent of the copyright
owner. Published by arrangement with Parachute Press, Inc.

Printed in U.S.A.

Busy Beavers

ERNIE the ELECTRICIAN

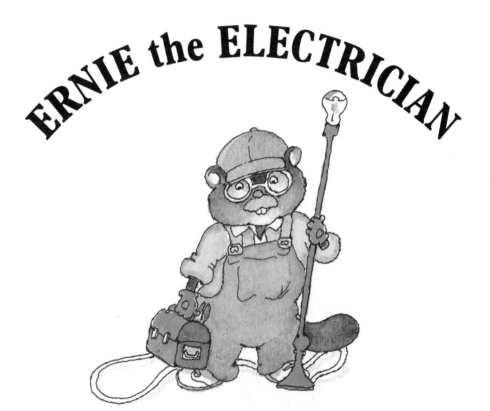

By Cathy East Dubowski
Illustrated by John Speirs

Ladybird Books

Here comes Ernie Beaver! He has a
lightning bolt painted on the side of his
truck. The truck is filled with tools and wires
and light bulbs.

Ernie is an electrician. He knows all about
electricity—that's the power that turns on
lights and runs machines.

Ernie will have to work fast today. Hocus Pocus the Magician is in town for one night only. Ernie wants to go to the show.

Ernie stops at Mr. DeLion's house. "My television won't turn on," says Mr. DeLion. "And my radio won't turn off!"

First, Ernie unplugs Mr. DeLion's radio so he won't get hurt by an electric shock. Then he goes to work on the radio. It needs a new switch.

Then Ernie checks Mr. DeLion's TV.
"Will I have to get a new one?" asks
Mr. DeLion.
"Oh, no," says Ernie. "Look. It just wasn't
plugged in!"

Ernie's next job is at a new house. He puts in all the new wires and switches and plugs. When the house is finished, the wires will be inside the walls. Nobody will see them, but they'll be there—working away!

Ernie's next job is at the Beaver Dam Shopping Center. He jumps into his truck and starts off.

Ernie stops at a red light. He waits for the green light. He waits and waits, and waits some more. But the green light never goes on. The police come. Something is wrong with the stoplight.

"I know how to fix it," says Ernie.

A green light— at last!

Ernie arrives at the shopping center.

"Thank goodness you're here," says Florida Flamingo. "Two of the letters in my sign have burned out, so now it says *Ball School*."

"Look at all these people. They want to learn how to play football, basketball, and volleyball. But I don't know how to play any of those games!"

Ernie fixes the sign. Now *all* the letters
light up. No wonder Florida was so upset!
Instead of *Ball School,* the sign now reads…

"Ballet school!" shout the ball players. "Yuck! Let's get out of here!"

"Oh, look, children," says Mrs. Lucy Goose. "*Just* what we were looking for."

Ernie has one last job to do.
He hooks up ceiling fans at
Dinah Hog's Deluxe Diner.
    "That's great!" says Dinah.
"How about a nice cool
lemonade?"
    "No thanks," says Ernie. "I
have to get ready for tonight's
magic show."

But when Ernie gets home, the phone is ringing. It's bad news. The lights have gone out at the Town Theater!

Ernie rushes over. The crowds are already
lining up to get in.

He rushes inside and goes to work.

"Hurry!" cries the manager. "If we don't get the lights fixed, we'll have to cancel the show."

At last—with only five minutes to show time—Ernie turns the lights back on.

"Ernie, you're terrific!" says the manager. "How would you like to see the show from a seat in the front row?"

"Thanks!" says Ernie. He hurries to his seat.

Soon, the music starts. The curtain goes up. Hocus Pocus, the famous magician, steps out onto the stage.

"Good evening, ladies and gentlemen," he says. "Thank you for coming. And now, if you please, may I have all the lights turned off? I always perform my magic by candlelight."

"Oh, no!" laughs Ernie.

Halfway through the show,
the manager whispers,
"Ernie, isn't the show great?"

But Ernie doesn't answer. The darkness of the auditorium and the gentle music have put the hard-working electrician to sleep!

Here are some of Ernie's favorite tools.

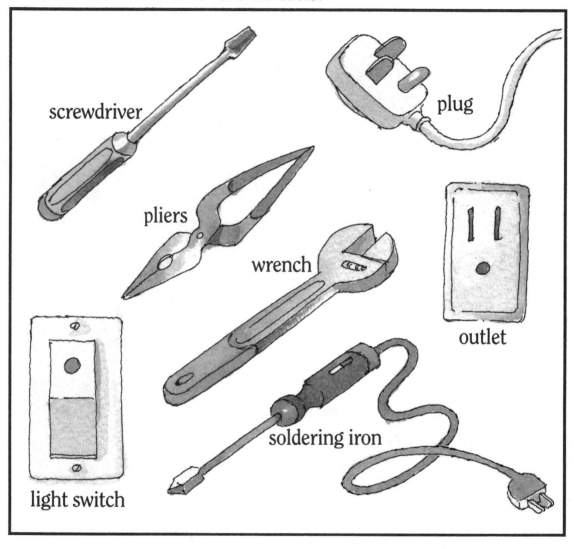

screwdriver

plug

pliers

wrench

outlet

light switch

soldering iron